CW00850821

A catalogue record for this book is available from the British Library

This version published by Ladybird Books Ltd
27 Wrights Lane London W8 5TZ
A Penguin Company
© LADYBIRD BOOKS LTD MCMXCIX
1 3 5 7 9 10 8 6 4 2
LADYBIRD and the device of a Ladybird are trademarks of Ladybird Books Ltd

Barney™

BJ™ and Baby Bop™'s Special Day

written by Stephen White
illustrated by Bill Langley

Ladybird

"Wake up Sissy. It's a new day!" BJ gave Baby Bop a gentle shake. Baby Bop yawned and smiled at her brother. Then she said, "BJ, today is a special day!"

"What's so special about it?" asked BJ.

Baby Bop hopped out of bed and said, "Today I want to do everything *just like you!*"

Baby Bop went to BJ's wardrobe
and found a hat and some shoes.
"Look," said Baby Bop, "I look
just like you!"
"You sure do," laughed BJ.
"You look
great!"

But Baby Bop could hardly walk in
BJ's shoes — *clump, clump, clump!*
And the hat kept falling down in
front of her eyes.
"Maybe I will do other things *just
like you*," she said.

After breakfast BJ played with his favourite toy truck.
"*Vroom, vroom!*" he said in a great big voice. "This truck is carrying lots of big heavy rocks."
Baby Bop said, "Oh, can I play? Please?"

Baby Bop put her blankey and her
favourite doll into a toy truck.
"Vroom, vroom!" she whispered
in a tiny voice. "This truck is
carrying a sleepy baby."
Then Baby Bop said, "See, BJ? I'm
playing *just like you!*"

Next BJ had fun building a tower with his toy bricks.
"Look how many I can stack," he said. "1...2...3...4...5...6...7...8...9...10!"
Baby Bop tried to build a tower too, but the bricks kept falling down.

So Baby Bop decided to line the bricks up neatly in a row. "Look," she said to BJ, "1...2...3...4...5...6...7...8...9...10! *Just like you!*"

Rat-a-tat-tat! Rat-a-tat-tat!
"I love playing my drum," said BJ
as he marched around the room.
Rat-a-tat-TAT-tat-TAT!

Baby Bop started banging pots
and pans with a big spoon. *Crash-
bang-boom! Crash-bang-boom!*
"I can play drums *just like you*!"
called Baby Bop over the noise.
BJ put his hands over his ears
and said, "Maybe we should play
outside."

"Whee!" said BJ. "Look at me. I can run in circles!"
BJ ran round the garden in great big circles. He was very fast.

"I can run fast, too!" said
Baby Bop.
And she spun round and round
until she felt so dizzy she almost
fell over.
"Look!" she giggled. "I can run in
circles *just like you!*"

"Zoom! I'm a jet pilot!" BJ said as he raced along the pavement on his bicycle.

Baby Bop followed on her
tricycle, ringing the bell:
Ring-a-ding! Ring-a-ding!
"Zoom! I'm a jet pilot with a
bell!" she called to her brother.
"*Just like you!*"

"I'm very good at jumping," said BJ—and he jumped over a big puddle.
"Look Sissy, I didn't even get wet!" he said.

But then BJ got a surprise.
Baby Bop jumped *into* the puddle!
SPLASH!
"I'm good at jumping too!" said
Baby Bop. "*Just like you!*"
BJ just laughed and said "Come
on. We'd better go and dry off."

When BJ and Baby Bop were clean and dry, they decided to have a snack.

"I really like pickles," said BJ, taking big bites. *Crunch! Crunch! Crunch!*

"I like pickles too, *just like you!*"
said Baby Bop.
She took a big bite. *Crunch!*
But the pickle was so sour that
Baby Bop made a funny face.
She put the pickle back down.
"I think I'm full," she said politely.

Then it was time for BJ's piano lesson.
"I practise every day, and every day I can play just a little bit better," he told Baby Bop.
BJ played a whole song with only a few mistakes.

Baby Bop played on her toy piano.
"I can practise *just like you!*" she
said.
BJ didn't know what song
Baby Bop was playing but he still
said, "That was lovely."

After having so much fun, BJ
thought it would be nice to
read a book. He sat
on the sofa and
quietly read
a story.
Baby Bop sat
on the sofa too.

She wanted to read but she was so sleepy that it was hard even to look at the pictures.

"I'm reading," Baby Bop said with a big yawn. "*Just like you!*"

"I think it's time for your sleep,"
BJ said to his little sister.
"Are you going to have a sleep
too?" asked Baby Bop sleepily.
"I don't think so," said BJ. "I'm
too big to have a sleep during
the day."

"When I'm bigger, I won't need a sleep either," yawned Baby Bop. "*Just like you.*"

Baby Bop climbed into her bed
and smiled a sleepy smile.
"I had a lovely time," she said.
"I had a lovely time too, Sissy,"
said BJ.
"*Just like you!*"